Written by Alva Sachs

Illustrated by Patricia Krebs

Three Wishes Publishing Company

Signature Book Printing - www.sbpbooks.com - Printed in the United States.
Third Printing September 2011

Layout by Marcie Gilbert and Patricia Krebs.
Jacket and cover design by Patricia Krebs.
Jacket photographs © by Marcie Gilbert.

First edition published 2007 by Three Wishes Publishing Company:
Three Wishes Publishing Company
26500 West Agoura Road, Suite 102-754
Calabasas, CA 91302
Phone: 818-878-0902
Fax: 818-878-1805
www.threewishespublishing.com

Library of Congress Cataloging-in-Publication Data:
Sachs, Alva
Circus fever / written by Alva Sachs ; illustrated by Patricia Krebs.
p. cm.
SUMMARY: Jessica is a nine-year-old girl with a big imagination and an even bigger love for the circus. To her delight, the circus is coming to town!.
Audience: Ages 5-9.
LCCN 2007904166
ISBN-13: 9780979638008
ISBN-10: 0979638003
1. Circus--Juvenile fiction. 2. Clowns--Juvenile fiction. [1. Circus--Fiction. 2. Clowns--Fiction.]
I. Krebs, Patricia, 1976- II. Title.
PZ7.S11852Cir 2007 [E]
QBI07-700136

The author wishes to thank the original three wishes -- Justin, Jessica, and Julie -- and Patricia Krebs and Marcie Gilbert for joining her on this journey.

This new chapter in my life is dedicated to Paul,
my loving husband and prince charming!

NEWS

Jessica peddled her bright blue bicycle as fast as she could.
She could see her house as she rounded the corner.
Her backpack was in her basket,
and under her arm was tucked the daily newspaper.

Jessica didn't take time to put her bicycle away today.

Instead, she ran straight to the kitchen.

"Mom, Mom!" Jessica shouted.

"Look at this! The circus is coming tomorrow!"

Her heart beat faster and faster while she hugged the headlines.

The fresh, warm smells of cotton candy and popcorn filled her head.

"Slow down, honey," Mom answered.

"But Mom, you don't understand.
I have been dreaming about this for a whole year!
I've saved all my money just for this."

"Yes, yes, I know, dear," Mom replied.
"Now that the circus is here,
we can make plans to go together,
just like we did last year."

"But, I want to go alone this year. I'm almost nine,
and I want to spend every day there."

"Oh, and I suppose you would rather live there too," smiled Mom.

A twinkle lit up in Jessica's eye.
Her rosy cheeks on her freckled face began to glow.

"Hurry and set the table. It's almost time for dinner."

"Sure thing, Mom," answered Jessica
as she carefully carried the dishes to the table.

Jessica sat at the table with Mom and Dad.
All she could think about was the circus.
"Jess, are you feeling all right?" Dad asked.
"You're not eating very much."

"I'm fine," sighed Jessica, "but may I go to my room?
I'm not very hungry."
With a nod of approval from her parents,
she dashed from the kitchen and ran straight to her bedroom.

The walls of her bedroom were covered with circus posters of all sorts. Elephants, lions, and tigers greeted Jessica the moment she entered.

Painted faces smiled down at her.
Each one had its own special look of delight.
Oh, how she loved the clowns!

Jessica stretched out on her bed and glanced from poster to poster.

She could hear the circus music all around her now.

The next thing she knew,
she was sitting at her mirror.
Jessica tied her hair up
with a fancy ribbon,
and opened a drawer
filled with Mom's left-over make-up.
She gathered the pretty colored cases,
and laid them in front of her.

The powder puff tickled
as she splashed it against her face.
Once the dust settled,
she opened her eyes.
Her freckles were still there!

"Oh, my gosh!" she exclaimed as she leaned closer to the mirror.
"Well, I guess I'll have to keep them there."
She picked up a fat black pencil,
and drew each freckle
into a perfect circle.

Jessica painted an arch above each eyebrow.
She picked up a shiny red tube of lipstick,
and turned its bottom, but nothing happened.
The tube was empty!
"Oh, no," she heard herself say, "there's no more red,
and that's all I need to finish!"

"Five minutes until show time!" a voice called out.

She tried turning the bottom of the lipstick again.
This time, up popped a fine fresh tube of red!
She circled her nose over and over again
until it looked three times its size.

Jessica reached for her wig.
She slipped on her flowered jacket over her suspenders.
Her blue and yellow shoes stuck out under her checkered pants.

A pretty purple flower
sprang out from the brim of her hat.
She pulled the cord on the flower,
just to make sure it was ready for the show.

Making her way towards the open tent,
Jessica glanced at herself in the mirror once more.
"How perfectly divine I look!" she thought
and winked at herself.

All three rings were busy
with acts of wonder and amazement.
Tigers jumped from stool to stool
at the crack of a whip.
Elephant trunks
were high
in the air,
turning,
twisting,
and bowing
with grace.
OOOs, AHHs,
and screams of delight
poured from the audience.

Without a net below them,
the trapeze artists swung to and fro.
Their glittering
costumes
floated
through the air.
The elephants
retreated,
and on
came the clowns.
They were running,
skipping,
and tripping
over each other.

Jessica crawled inside
a tiny house
and screamed
out a window.
It was a cry
for HELP!
Suddenly,
flames surrounded
her house!

A siren rang in the distance,
and along came the Circus Fire Truck.

The clowns pulled
and tugged
at the hoses,
but no water would come out.

The clowns placed a ladder against the window.

Jessica
slid
down
the ladder,

and landed safely on the ground.

The clowns danced
and stumbled about,
trying to put out
the roaring fire.

Jessica glared at the fire.

She lifted her arms to the air for silence.

A hush fell over the crowd.

All eyes were on this tiny, adorable,

freckle-faced clown.

Jessica tilted her head,
and pulled the cord
of the flower
on her hat.
Water squirted
everywhere.
The fire was out
in a flash!

Thunderous applause rocked the tent.

Jessica bowed, and the clowns dragged her from the ring.

"Thank you, thank you," Jessica sang out.

"Jessica, honey, it's time to go to sleep now," Mom said gently.

"Remember, we are going to see the circus tomorrow."

CIRCUS
CIRCUS

Jessica looked up
at Mom's smiling eyes.
"I know
Mom,
and I
can't wait
to go
back!"

For Audrey –
dream Big!
[illegible]